A Viking Easy-to-Read

MY PONY JACK
★ AT THE ★
HORSE SHOW

By CARI MEISTER

Illustrated by AMY YOUNG

For Jameson—C.M.

To the Usual Suspects—A.Y.

VIKING

Published by Penguin Group

Penguin Young Readers Group, 345 Hudson Street, New York, New York 10014, U.S.A.

Penguin Books Ltd, Registered Offices: 80 Strand, London WC2R 0RL, England

First published in 2006 by Viking, a division of Penguin Young Readers Group

1   3   5   7   9   10   8   6   4   2

LIBRARY OF CONGRESS CATALOGING-IN-PUBLICATION DATA
Meister, Cari.
My pony Jack at the horse show / by Cari Meister ; illustrations by Amy Young.
p. cm.
Summary: Easy-to-read, rhyming text follows Lacy and her
pony, Jack, as they compete in a horse show.
ISBN 0-670-05919-6 (hardcover)
[1. Horse shows—Fiction. 2. Ponies—Fiction.
3. Stories in rhyme.] I. Young, Amy, ill. II. Title.
PZ8.3.M5514myad 2006
[E]—dc22

2005022810

Manufactured in China
Set in Bookman

Viking® and Easy-to-Read® are registered trademarks of Penguin Group (USA) Inc.

Today is the horse show.

We have to get ready.

Jack needs a bath.

"Whoa, Jack! Stand steady."

I braid his mane
and make it neat.

I put shiny stuff
all over his feet.

"Jack, you look great!

And so do I.

The trailer is waiting.

Time to go! Bye-bye!"

There are so many people!

There are so many horses!

This place is too big!

There are three jumping courses!

"Lacy!" calls Annie.

"We are over here.

"Take a deep breath.

Now wipe your tears.

"Just do like your lessons.
You will be fine.

Put on a smile,

and get in that line."

The judge calls us in.

We trot right away.

"Canter your ponies!"

Look out for that bay!

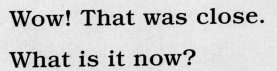

Wow! That was close.

What is it now?

Sitting trot?

I forget how!

I look at Annie.

She gives me a sign.

I must be okay.

"All horses in line!"

Second place!

"Good job, Jack!

Here is your ribbon.

Here is your snack.

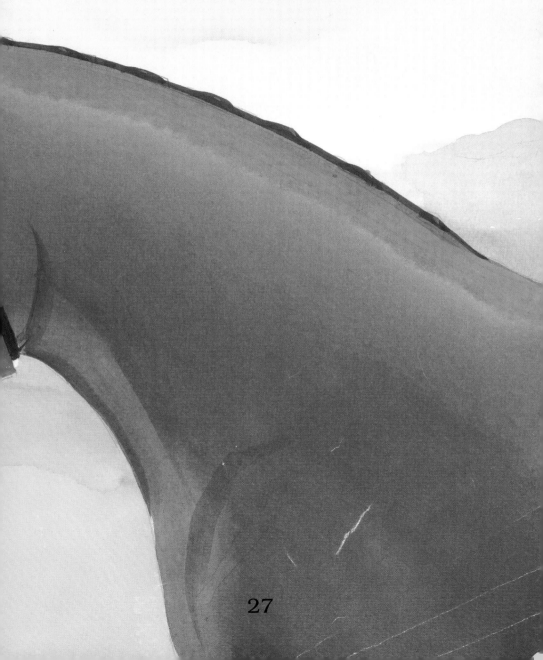

"Into the trailer, Jack.

You know the way.

"It is time to go home.

What a fun day!"

• PONY WORDS •

BAY: a dark-skinned pony with a dark brown to reddish-brown coat and a black mane and tail.

CANTER: a three-beat gait that is slower than a gallop (a gallop is the fastest a pony can run).

HORSE SHOW: a contest for horses, ponies, and riders.

JUMPING COURSE: a set of jumps or other obstacles set up for a pony and rider to jump over.

SHINY STUFF: hoof hardener; like nail polish for a pony's hooves.

SITTING TROT: the rider does not move up and down in the saddle, but stays "sitting."

TRAILER: the vehicle that a pony rides in that is pulled behind a car or truck.

TROT: a two-beat gait that is slower than a canter.